Fancy NANCY

Tea for Two

Based on *Fancy Nancy* written by Jane O'Connor

Cover illustration by Robin Preiss Glasser

Interior illustrations by Carolyn Bracken

HARPER FESTIVAL
An Imprint of HarperCollinsPublishers

HarperFestival is an imprint of HarperCollins Publishers.

Fancy Nancy: Tea for Two
Text copyright © 2012 by Jane O'Connor
Illustrations copyright © 2012 by Robin Preiss Glasser
For information address HarperCollins Children's Books, a division of HarperCollins Publishers, 195 Broadway, New York, NY 10007.
www.harpercollinschildrens.com
Library of Congress catalog card number: 2011926075
ISBN 978-0-06-123597-9
Book design by Sean Boggs
16   SCP   20 19 18 17 16 15
❖
First Edition

Ooh la la! There's a message from my best friend, Bree, in our special mail basket. It says, "Come quick! I have something to show you!"

The mail basket is set up on a rope that runs between our houses.
This way we can always stay in touch.

I write back a message. It says, "I will be there in a jiffy." (That's fancy for right away.) Off it goes in the basket.

Then I wake my doll Marabelle from her nap and head next door.

As soon as I arrive, Bree says, "Close your eyes and count to three."
"*Un, deux, trois.*" I love counting in French!

When I open my eyes, Bree is holding a tray with a fancy tea set on it.
There is a teapot, a sugar bowl, a creamer, and two cups with saucers.
"Ooh! How elegant!" I say.

"My aunt gave it to me," Bree explains.
"She and my mom used to play tea party with it."

"This tea set is extra special," Bree says. "It's real china, not plastic. That's why there are a few little chips."

We decide to have a tea party right away—a doll tea party. Isn't it lucky I brought Marabelle with me?

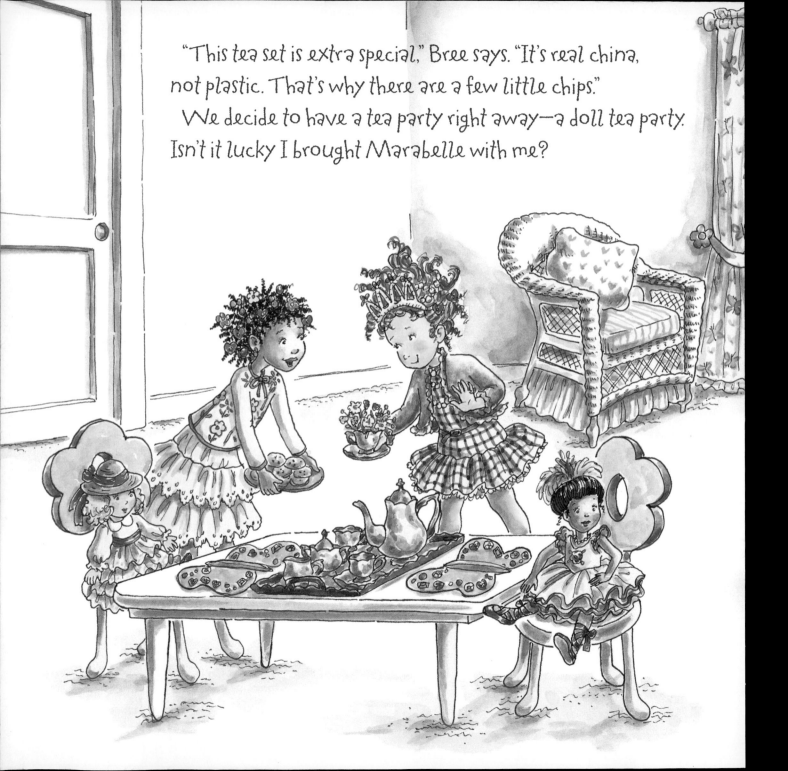

We put out place mats, set the table, stick some flowers in a vase, and voilà—it's party time.

Bree wants her doll Chiffon to be hostess first.
That's fair—the tea set is Bree's, after all.

"Darling, would you care for some tea?" Chiffon asks.
"Oui, oui. Yes, please," Marabelle answers. Marabelle
has absolutely exquisite manners. (That means her
manners are just about perfect.)

The dolls sip their tea in a very dainty, fancy way.

When they are done, I say, "Now it's Marabelle's turn to pour."
I start to reach for the teapot.

"No!" says Bree. She pushes my hand away. "Chiffon is still the hostess."
That is not fair! "Marabelle deserves a turn," I say.

I reach to take the teapot from Bree. Then something horrible happens. The teapot goes flying...

...and when it lands,
its lid breaks into two pieces!
"My tea set is wrecked!" Bree shouts.

"It was an accident," I say. "And anyway, the teapot already had a chip in it."
Bree flops on her bed and covers her face. "Go home. I don't want to play."

"Fine. I am leaving, and I'm not coming back—au revoir!"

Then Marabelle and I storm out of Bree's house and back to mine.

At home, I keep looking outside my window to see if Bree sent a message saying she's sorry for how mean she was. But the mail basket is empty.

During dinner my mom asks if something is wrong,
so I tell everyone what happened.
   My dad says, "Even though it was an accident,
it was your fault the teapot broke."

My mom asks, "Did you say you were sorry?"

"Well, not exactly," I say.

"That's what you need to do," Mom says.

My parents are right. But what if Bree stays mad at me forever?

The next morning, I go over to Bree's house to apologize, which is the fancy word for saying sorry. But when she answers the door, all I do is burst into tears.

Bree starts crying then too. "I'm sorry I hogged the tea set."

"And I am so sorry I broke the teapot. I never should have grabbed it. I was scared we weren't going to be best friends anymore," I tell Bree.

"Me too!" Bree says.

Then we embrace, which is fancy for hug.

And guess what? The teapot is already repaired, which means it's fixed and fine again—just like our friendship.